THE MOUSIER THE MERRIER!

by **Eleanor May** • Illustrated by **Deborah Melmon**

THE KANE PRESS / NEW YORK

For Alanna and Aeva
—E.M.

Library of Congress Cataloging-in-Publication Data

May, Eleanor.
The mousier the merrier / by Eleanor May ; illustrated by Deborah Melmon.
   p. cm. — (Mouse math)
Summary: Albert and Wanda want to invite a friend over to play on a rainy day, but they soon count
fifteen mice in the walls of the People House.
   ISBN 978-1-57565-440-9 (pbk. : alk. paper) — ISBN 978-1-57565-441-6
(e-book) — ISBN 978-1-57565-447-8 (library reinforced binding : alk. paper)
   [1. Mice—Fiction. 2. Counting.] I. Melmon, Deborah, ill. II. Title.
   PZ7.M4513Mou 2012
   [E]—dc23
                    2011048823

1 3 5 7 9 10 8 6 4 2

First published in the United States of America in 2012 by Kane Press, Inc.
Printed in the United States of America
WOZ0712

Book Design: Edward Miller

Mouse Math is a trademark of Kane Press, Inc.

Visit us online at **www.kanepress.com**

Like us on Facebook
facebook.com/kanepress

Follow us on Twitter
@KanePress

Dear Parent/Educator,

"I can't do math." Every child (or grownup!) who says these words has at some point along the way felt intimidated by math. For young children who are just being introduced to the subject, we wanted to create a world in which math was not simply numbers on a page, but a part of life—an adventure!

Enter Albert and Wanda, two little mice who live in the walls of a People House. Children will be swept along with this irrepressible duo and their merry band of friends as they tackle mouse-sized problems and dilemmas. (And sometimes *cat-sized* problems and dilemmas!)

Each book in the **MOUSE MATH**™ series provides a fresh take on a basic math concept. The mice discover solutions as they, for instance, use position words while teaching a pet snail to do tricks or count the alarmingly large number of friends they've invited over on a rainy day—and, lo and behold, they are doing math!

Math educators who specialize in early childhood learning used their expertise to make sure each title would be as helpful as possible to young kids—and to their parents and teachers. Fun activities at the end of the books and on our website encourage children to think and talk about math in ways that will make each concept clear and memorable.

As with our award-winning Math Matters® series, our aim is to captivate children's imaginations by drawing them into the story, and so into the math at the heart of each adventure. It is our hope that kids will want to hear and read the **MOUSE MATH** stories again and again and that, as they grow up, they will approach math with enthusiasm and see it as an invaluable tool for navigating the world they live in.

Sincerely,

Joanne Kane

Joanne E. Kane
Publisher

It was a rainy day. Albert was bored.

No outside games today. No Cheese Tag.
No Hide-and-Go-Squeak.

His friends were all holed up in their own homes in the walls of the People House.

"I wish I had someone to play with," Albert complained.

"Why don't you go see if Leo can come over?"
Mom asked. "You two can play a game."

6

Albert's sister, Wanda, looked up from her book.
"Can I ask Lucy, too?"

Mom smiled. "Of course! The mousier the merrier."

Albert and Wanda scampered down the passageway.
Then suddenly, they heard—

MEOW

9

It was their friend Charlie.

"You didn't fool me," Albert grumbled.

"Where are you going?" Charlie asked.

"To see if Leo and Lucy can come over and play," Wanda said.

"Can I come over too?"

"Sure," Albert said. "But no more meowing. You might scare my mom."

Charlie went to ask his parents if he could go play.
Albert and Wanda hurried on.

"Four mice were going to play at our house,"
Wanda said. "You, me, Lucy, and Leo. Now we'll
have five. We didn't ask if we could invite Charlie."

Albert smiled. "You heard Mom—the mousier
the merrier!"

A delicious smell drifted through an open door.
Ronald and Rachel were making cheese soup
for lunch.

"Want to come over and play?" Albert asked.

"We'd love to!" Rachel said.

"After we wash the dishes," Ronald reminded her.

"There were going to be five of us," Wanda said.
"Rachel makes six. Ronald makes seven."

"Yes!" Albert said. "Isn't that great?"

16

They met up with the Mousely triplets next.

Albert invited them, too.

"Eight, nine, ten." Wanda groaned.
"Where are we going to put ten mice?"

Albert shrugged cheerfully.
He ran on ahead.

Melody was practicing with her new band, Mousetrap.
Albert invited all four of them.

19

"Eleven, twelve, thirteen, *fourteen*? Albert! That's TOO MANY MICE!"

"The mousier the merrier!" Albert reminded her.

Wanda covered her eyes.

Finally, they reached Leo and Lucy's house.

"Can we bring our cousin Fred?" Leo asked.

"The mousier the merrier!" Albert said.

Wanda just moaned.

On the way home, the four band members joined them. . . .

Then the Mousely triplets . . .

. . . Rachel and Ronald . . .

. . . and Charlie.

"Wow," Charlie said. "That's a lot of mice!"

Albert looked around and gulped.
All he had wanted was a friend or two
to make a rainy day more fun.
But *fifteen* mice?

What in the world would Mom say?

Mom opened the door.
She looked at all the mice.
She looked at Albert.

"You know what I always say . . ."

"THE MOUSIER THE MERRIER!"

And fifteen mice ran outside to play in the sun.

The Mousier the Merrier! supports children's understanding of **numbers and counting**, important topics in early math learning. Use the activities below to extend the math topic and to reinforce children's early reading skills.

ENGAGE

Remind children that the cover of a book can tell them a lot about the story inside.

▶ Read the title aloud and direct children's attention to the illustration. Ask: *What do you think the story is about?* Ask children if they have ever heard the phrase "the more the merrier!" What do they think it means? Encourage them to tell about times when they've been merry. (You may want to talk about the meaning of the adjectives *merry*, *merrier*, and *merriest*.)

LOOK BACK

▶ As you re-read the story aloud, tell children to listen carefully for the refrain "the mousier the merrier." Invite them to say the refrain aloud each time it appears in the story. Can they predict when Albert will repeat the refrain?

▶ Direct children to pages 6 and 7. Ask: *Whom does Albert want to invite? Whom does Wanda want to invite? How do you think Mom feels about this? How do you know?*

▶ Look at page 16. Ask: *How many mice are going to play?* Encourage children to describe what Albert does on page 17. Ask: *What do you think Wanda will say?* (Possible answer: We were counting on seven mice, and now we'll have three more!)

 ## TRY THIS!

▶ Write the questions below on the board or on a large sheet of paper.

▶ Have children look at the illustration on pages 24–25 as you read each question aloud. (Printable art is also available at www.kanepress.com/mousemath-counting.html.)

▶ Invite a volunteer to write the correct number next to each question.

1. How many mice are there altogether?
2. How many mice are wearing hats?
3. How many mice are gray?
4. How many mice have spotted fur?
5. How many mice have stripes on their shirts?
6. How many mice are nibbling on cookies?

Challenge

You may wish to extend the activity by asking questions such as:
How many mice have spotted fur AND stripes on their shirts?
How many mice are wearing hats AND black shirts?

🐭 THINK!

▶ Tell children to listen closely as a volunteer retells *The Mousier the Merrier!* in his or her own words. Have children "tally up" or keep track as the mice are invited. (Be sure to include Albert and Wanda in the tally!) When the retelling is finished, count together to be sure the total number of mice is the same as in the book (15).

▶ Print a copy of the page of mice from www.kanepress.com/mousemath-counting.html for each child. Give them the following instructions:

  • *Pretend you are Albert or Wanda. Think of a special event you'd like to have— such as a cheese party, a sleepover, or a camping trip. What are some of the fun things you would do? How many mice would you invite?*
  • *Color the mice and cut them out. Now glue them to a clean sheet of paper and draw a picture of your event!*

  Bonus: *When your picture is done, carefully count up all the mice. Did you end up inviting the number of mice you intended to?*

▶ Encourage children to share their stories.

◆ **FOR MORE ACTIVITIES** ◆
visit **www.kanepress.com/mousemath-activities.html**